THE TRANSFORMERS™— Robots in Disguise!

They came from Cybertron—a planet of machines—where war raged for thousands of years between the noble Autobots and the evil Decepticons.

NOW THE BATTLE OF THESE POWERFUL ROBOTS IS YOUR BATTLE!

ONLY YOU can protect the earth from the evil destruction of the Decepticons!

Read the directions at the bottom of each page. Then decide what the Autobots should do next.

If you decide correctly, the Autobots will triumph! If you make the wrong choices, the unspeakable evil of the Decepticons will rule the world!

Hurry! The adventure begins on page 1.

THE TRANSFORMERS™

Attack of the Insecticons

by Lynn Beach

BALLANTINE BOOKS • NEW YORK

Library of Congress Catalog Card Number: 85-90608

ISBN: 0-345-32671-7

Editorial Services by Parachute Press, Inc.

Illustrated by William Schmidt

Designed by Gene Siegel

Manufactured in the United States of America

First Edition: December 1985

10 9 8 7 6 5 4

THE TRANSFORMERS™
Attack of the Insecticons

Varoom!!

The sound of a powerful motor echoes deep within a cave somewhere in the Pacific Northwest. Hanging from the ceiling, stalactites vibrate from the sound. A racetrack has been cleared on the rocky floor.

Around the outside of the track stand the Autobots. With them are their human friends Sparkplug Witwicky and his son, Buster.

They are watching a large red van speed around the track. It is Ironhide, the oldest and toughest of the Autobots. He is testing the Sun-Pak, an experimental solar battery designed by Sparkplug. They are deep underground so that the test will be secret. The Autobots need fuel as much as humans need food. If this battery works as well as Sparkplug says, it could be the answer to the Autobots' prayers!

Optimus Prime, the leader of the Autobots, is elated. "Twenty-three hours and still going strong!" he says.

Ratchet has been keeping a close eye on the test. If something goes wrong, he's the Autobot fix-it man. "Hey, Ironhide," he calls to the red van, "how are you feeling? Have your old gears started to wear out yet?"

"Go chew on a microchip!" shouts Ironhide as he whizzes by. "I have never felt better!"

Sparkplug checks his stopwatch. "According to my calculations, he should have full power for another hour."

....

Turn to page 2.

1

"With the Sun-Pak, just one hour of sunlight can provide an Autobot with all the energy he needs for a full day," says Optimus Prime. "You are a genius, Sparkplug!"

"I'm just a good mechanic," the human says modestly.

"This could be the end of our constant search for fuel," Optimus Prime goes on. "It could be the key to defeating the Decepticons!"

At the mention of the Decepticons, Buster cannot help shivering. He is proud of his father. But he knows how evil the Decepticons are.

"He still has forty minutes to go," says Optimus Prime.

What he doesn't know is that time may be running out for the Autobots.

Unknown to the humans and Autobots, they are not alone in the cave. Kickback, the evil Insecticon, has been watching and listening. The grasshopper-like being also realizes how valuable the Sun-Pak could be.

The Decepticons must have this battery, he thinks to himself. Megatron will reward me well!

....

Go on to page 3.

He does not wait for the test to be finished. He slips out of the cave. Then he transmits a message to top-secret Decepticon headquarters.

"Megatron isn't here," answers Starscream, the powerful Decepticon. "He and some of the others are raiding a human power facility. What have you found, Insecticon?"

Kickback tells Starscream about the test of the Sun-Pak.

This is my chance to take command! thinks Starscream. He turns to the Decepticons remaining at headquarters. "Decepticons," he commands, "prepare to attack the Autobots!"

Back in the cavern, Ironhide is still going strong.

All the Autobots begin to cheer. They cannot hear a distant rumble outside the cave. It is the rumble of jet fighters approaching. But these are not ordinary jet fighters. It is a raiding party of Decepticons, led by the silver jet, Starscream!

Now Optimus Prime calls out, "Ten seconds!"

The other Autobots take up the count: "Nine, eight, seven, six..."

Turn to page 4.

At that moment rocks begin to fall and the cave floor starts shaking. Then an unimaginable sight: a jet fighter plane flies into the cave!

"The Decepticons!" cries Optimus Prime. Quickly he pushes Sparkplug and Buster into a crevice away from the fighting. "Autobots, defend yourselves!" He aims his laser rifle at Starscream and fires.

"Nice try, insulation-breath!" snarls Starscream. Turning sharply, he drops a load of cluster bombs. The bombs miss the Autobots, but they shatter the stalactites. Large chunks of rock fall everywhere.

Other Decepticons have now entered the cave. Kickback rakes the Autobots with his submachine gun. Rumbles and groundwaves shake the cavern.

"Give up, you tin-plated trash cans!" commands Starscream. "Give up before we bury you under a hundred tons of rock!"

Just then Bumblebee, the smallest of the Autobots, rolls up to Optimus Prime. "Optimus Prime," he says, "the fighting has opened a hole in the back of the cave! I checked it out. There seems to be a tunnel to the surface. Maybe we could get out that way!"

Go on to page 5.

4

Optimus Prime thinks quickly. "Good work, Bumblebee," he says. "Even though we outnumber the Decepticons, all of us are low on fuel. I hate to retreat in the middle of a battle, but..."

Another blast rocks the cave. The Autobots are fighting bravely. But the weapons and falling rocks are causing dents and shattered photocells. Optimus Prime knows it is only a matter of time before someone is seriously hurt.

What should Optimus Prime do now? Should he stand and continue to fight the evil Decepticons?

Or would it be safer to retreat into the tunnel and return to fight another day?

If you think Optimus Prime should stand and fight now, turn to page 20.

If you think it would be wiser to retreat, turn to page 40.

"Take the tunnel on the right," Optimus Prime orders. "Autobots, advance!"

Bumblebee leads the way. It is dark, so he turns on his headlights.

"It's spooky in here," says Buster. "And what is that buzzing noise?"

"Don't worry," says Bumblebee. "We'll be out soon."

But the tunnel keeps going. The buzzing grows louder. The tunnel twists and turns, deep into the mountain.

This must be the wrong passage, Optimus Prime thinks. "Autobots," he orders, "reverse course!"

But at that moment there is a rumbling noise. A rock slide begins to rush down the tunnel. The Autobots cannot turn around.

"Hold on!" cries Bumblebee. Buster and Sparkplug hold tight. Bumblebee and the other Autobots slide down...down...down.

With a deafening crash, they reach the bottom of a canyon. The path they had been following is no longer there. The entire corridor has caved in!

"Check for injuries!" cries Ratchet. One by one the Autobots report.

"Minor dents," says Mirage.

Turn to page 8.

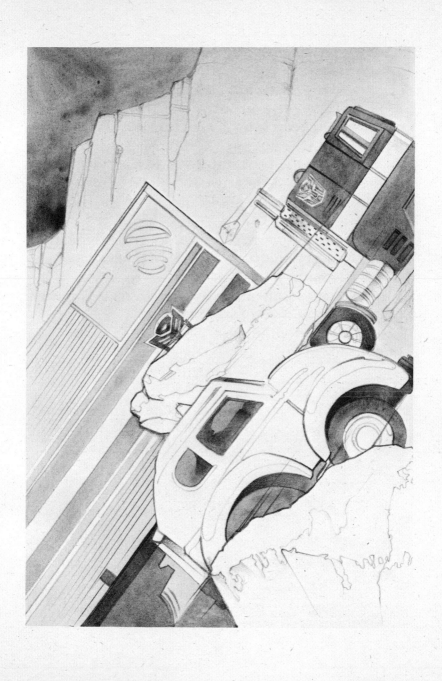

"One headlight out," says Bumblebee. "Are you guys all right?" he asks Sparkplug and Buster.

"Shook up—but fine," Sparkplug answers.

The Autobots transform into their robot forms and begin the search for a way out.

"What do we do now?" grumbles Ironhide.

"Don't worry," says Optimus Prime. "We'll find another way out. At least we're safe."

"Don't be too sure about that," says a harsh, metallic voice.

Now the Autobots look around through the dust and gloom. For the first time they realize what the buzzing noise is.

Standing over them, aiming his grenade launcher, is the terrifying Insecticon Shrapnel.

"Welcome to the nest of the Insecticons," he chuckles.

Turn to page 34.

"I'm not afraid of Megatron," says Shrapnel. "With the Sun-Pak I will be more powerful than he is."

At that moment a dark shadow slips out of the trees. The Insecticons do not see it. But Mirage and Buster instantly understand what has happened.

"That was Ravage!" whispers Mirage. "He's Megatron's top spy. He heard about the Sun-Pak. And now he must be taking the news to Megatron!"

"Then Megatron's Decepticons will be here any minute," says Buster. "What can we do?"

"We'll have to move fast," says Mirage. "We can try to get the Sun-Pak before the Decepticons arrive—"

"But there are only two of us against all the Insecticons," says Buster. "Besides, we promised Optimus Prime we wouldn't do anything on our own."

"Promises sometimes have to be broken," says Mirage. "We'd better make a decision. Time is running out."

What should Mirage and Buster do?

If you think they should forget their promise to Optimus Prime and try to steal back the Sun-Pak, turn to page 30.

If you think they should call Optimus Prime and hope he gets here in time, turn to page 11.

"A Decepticon's word is worthless!" says Optimus Prime. "Nice try, Starscream. Now prepare to become scrap metal!"

Smokescreen aims his disrupter rifle. He is ready to bring a quick end to the evil jet fighter.

But at just that moment, the other Decepticons counterattack. Thundercracker's deafening sonic boom throws Smokescreen to the floor. Fire bombs, rockets, and magnetic blasts rock the Autobots.

"Autobots—defend yourselves!" gasps Optimus Prime. He attacks his foes with the laser rifle. But he can feel his energy slipping away.

"So," the evil voice of Starscream comes from above where he hovers. "You may have wounded me, but I'll have the last laugh, Prime. You can have the Sun-Pak, but the Decepticons will have its inventor!"

With that he swoops down to where Sparkplug and Buster are hiding. With one quick move he grasps Sparkplug in his tractor beam. Then he flies from the cave, the other Decepticons behind him.

Turn to page 50.

10

Quickly Mirage radios to Autobot headquarters. "Come prepared for heavy fighting," he tells Optimus Prime. "We're expecting the Decepticons soon!"

Mirage is right. It's a very short time before the roar of jet planes is heard.

"The Decepticons are on their way!" Mirage says. "Let's hide in those rocks over there."

The Decepticons arrive, transform into robots, and enter the deadly forest.

"What's this Ravage tells me about a solar battery?" Megatron demands in his booming voice.

"I don't know what you're talking about," says Shrapnel. He tries to hide the Sun-Pak behind his back.

"Liar!" thunders Megatron. He knocks Shrapnel to the ground with a blast from his fusion cannons. "You and all the Insecticons must be punished! I order you to—"

But at that moment the sound of car engines signals that the *Autobots* have arrived!

"The Autobots!" cries Megatron. "They must have tracked Shrapnel." He thinks for a moment. "This may prove to be the luckiest day of our lives," he says. "They don't know we are here. They are rolling into a trap. Decepticons, prepare your weapons. Fire on my command!"

Turn to page 33.

11

Quickly Optimus Prime gives the orders. Before Starscream knows what is happening, he is the object of an all-out attack!

"Take that, you flying fathead!" cries the leader of the Autobots. He aims his laser gun and fires in a steady burst.

Starscream turns sharply to avoid the devastating light beams. He narrowly misses a large stalactite. The other Decepticons attack—but without Starscream's command they are disorganized. Their shots often miss their marks. Now the Autobot Smokescreen shoots missiles from his shoulder-mounted launchers. The missiles burst into sharp pieces all around Starscream. They produce thousands of radio signals and microwaves.

"*Aaaargh!*" screams the evil Decepticon. "My guidance systems are shattered! Stop! Stop! I surrender!" He is flying in circles and seems about to crash.

"Don't trust him," says Smokescreen. "One blast of my disrupter rifle will bring him down for good!"

Turn to page 69.

They decide to contact Megatron. So they sneak over to a deserted corner of the museum. In a few seconds, Blaster has set up a communications link with Decepticon headquarters. Buster's heart is pounding when he asks to speak to Megatron.

After a moment Megatron's voice booms from the speaker. "What do you want with Megatron, human?"

"I want to make a trade with you," says Buster. He tries not to sound nervous.

"A trade? Don't make me laugh!" says Megatron. "What Megatron wants, he takes!"

"Maybe so," says Buster. "But I think you'll be interested in this. What if I told you I have proof that Starscream is a traitor?"

"Impossible!" says Megatron.

"Don't be too sure. I have a tape that proves it!" says Buster. He is feeling more confident every minute.

Megatron doesn't speak again for a moment. "I don't know what sort of human trick this is," he says. "But I might be amused to hear your so-called tape. What do you want in return?"

Go on to page 15.

"My father's life," says Buster. Quickly he explains that Sparkplug has been captured by Starscream and Bombshell. He doesn't mention the Sun-Pak.

"I might be willing to make such a trade," says Megatron. "But first I must hear the tape. Transmit it to me now. Then we'll talk again."

"No," says Buster. "Order Starscream to release my father. Then I'll give you the tape."

"How dare you presume to set conditions for Megatron!" thunders the Decepticon. "Transmit the tape now. That's my final offer!"

Quickly Buster and Blaster confer.

If you think they should trust Megatron and play him the tape, turn to page 26.

If you think they should refuse to play the tape until Sparkplug is released, turn to page 46.

15

Optimus Prime knows it's up to him to break the standoff and face Megatron—one-on-one. He approaches Megatron. Just as the Decepticon is about to fire, Optimus Prime holds up his hand. "Halt!" he commands.

"What do you mean, halt?" says Megatron. "We're in the middle of a battle."

"A battle of unnecessary destruction, Megatron," says Optimus Prime. "The casualties are heavy on both sides. Let our forces withdraw!"

"Are you proposing a truce, coward?" sneers Megatron.

"Not at all," says Optimus Prime. "I'm proposing a duel—between you and me. Whoever wins gets the Sun-Pak—if you have the guts!"

Megatron thinks for a moment. "Why not?" he says. "There's no way you can beat me, Prime. And when the battle is over, you will finally know who is master! Decepticons, withdraw!"

Optimus Prime nods in agreement. "Autobots, withdraw!"

Go on to page 17.

As the Autobots and Decepticons back away from the battle, the ancient foes face each other. Both Optimus Prime and Megatron use every weapon in their possession. Laser gun and fusion cannon clash again and again. Though both are growing weaker, they continue to fight with skill and cunning.

"They're perfectly matched," says Smokescreen.

"I agree," says Mirage. "In fact, I suspect that the outcome of this fight can be determined only by fate."

Mirage is right. To discover the outcome of this even fight, flip a coin.

If it comes up heads, turn to page 52.
If it comes up tails, turn to page 37.

17

For the next two hours Mirage and Buster travel through the twists and turns of mountain roads. The ultrasonic signals grow louder.

"This is it," Mirage says at last. They are in front of a forest of dead and rotting trees. They can barely see through the twisted and gnarled branches, but they can hear the sound of buzzing and metallic voices.

Stealthily, human and Autobot approach the deadly forest. The branches are like bony arms that grab them as they walk. Mirage activates his electro-disrupter. Instantly he and Buster appear to be part of the background of rotting trees and vines. "The illusion will only last six minutes," the Autobot whispers. "We'd better get what we need by then."

He and Buster reach a clearing where the Insecticons are standing in a circle, talking. Buster cannot help it—he shudders at their evil appearance. Luckily, the Insecticons don't see him.

"Look at this, my brother Insecticons," Shrapnel is saying. He is holding the Sun-Pak. "With this device we will no longer need fuel. We will be the most powerful beings on this planet."

"I don't know," says Kickback. "What if Megatron finds out that we have it?"

Turn to page 9.

19

"We will never give in to the Decepticons!" cries Optimus Prime. "We'll stand and fight!"

The battle continues to rage. There are many more Autobots than Decepticons. But the Decepticons are all fully fueled.

"Had enough, Autobots?" sneers Starscream. "Or do you really want to be turned into junk?"

Optimus Prime doesn't bother to answer. Starscream seems overconfident. And the evil jet fighter is having trouble flying in the cave. Optimus Prime now thinks that he may be able to trap his foe. Perhaps this is the chance to get rid of Starscream once and for all!

All he needs to do is order all the Autobots to turn their weapons on Starscream. But that would mean leaving the Autobots and humans unprotected from the other Decepticons.

Is that plan too risky? What should Optimus Prime do?

If you think he should order an attack on Starscream, turn to page 12.

If you think he should continue to battle all of the Decepticons, turn to page 32.

Beachcomber takes a last look at the beauty of the underground cavern. Then he continues straight ahead on the path.

He has entered a narrow, twisting tunnel. Every few yards he checks his sensors. They tell him that he is not getting any closer to the surface. But at least he isn't getting any farther from it.

Or is he?

The passage has begun to twist and turn. Side paths lead off from it. And now Beachcomber's sensors are beginning to give him conflicting data.

His magnetic sensors tell him that he is on a route straight up to the surface. But his seismic sensors indicate that he is deep within the mountain.

I must have entered an area of magnetic disturbance, he thinks. Well, I still have my sonic probe. He tries the sonic probe, but it is too weak to penetrate the dense rock.

Now he is feeling weaker himself. With sudden panic, he realizes that he has spent too much time in this passage.

Turn to page 22.

Beachcomber turns around and starts to go back the way he came. But the way no longer looks familiar, and his sensors are no longer working. He turns sharply to the left and comes upon the terrifying, towering figure of Megatron.

"Well, what have we here?" Megatron says with a sneer. "We're just on our way to join your friends for a chat—with these." Megatron points to his fusion cannons and blasters. His horrible laugh is the last sound Beachcomber hears as he is blasted out of Megatron's way, out of the cavern, and out of the story.

We'll skip the horrible details of the Autobots' defeat. You can picture it—the blasts, the cries, the fierce Insecticons' sting. Had enough? Let's just say this is . . .

THE END

Kickback attacks. His submachine gun finds its target. Beachcomber tries to fight back—but he is no match for the quick Insecticon.

It looks like the end—for Beachcomber, for the Sun-Pak, and for the Autobots.

Is it?

Turn to page 62 and find out.

The mighty Megatron appears before the terrified Decepticons. "It doesn't matter how I found you," says Megatron. "What matters is that I *have* found you. And I know what you're up to, traitor!" There is a loud *click*, and the tape recording begins to play. Starscream's voice is unmistakable: "*At long last the Decepticons will obey me as their rightful leader.*"

"You don't understand, Megatron," Starscream babbles desperately. "I was only joking. I've never wanted to do anything but serve you. Ask Bombshell! He knows I'm loyal! He's been with me the whole time!"

"It's true that I've been with Starscream, Mighty Megatron," says the Insecticon. "But I have been trying to talk him out of his treasonous plans!"

"Liar!" shouts Starscream. "I'll get you for this, you tin-plated grasshopper!"

"Silence!" thunders Megatron. "I have suspected that you plot behind my back, Starscream. But at last I have proof. That proof is much more important than this miserable human. Release him! And you return to headquarters immediately for reprogramming—or you will feel the might of the entire Decepticon force!"

Go on to page 25.

"I'll escort the traitor to headquarters, Mighty Megatron," says Bombshell eagerly. He releases Sparkplug, as Megatron ordered. Then he transforms into his insect form, and he and Starscream leave the museum. Megatron looks at Sparkplug for an instant—as if he was going to change his mind about keeping his word—but then he turns and goes.

"Over here, Pop," calls Buster. Still carrying Blaster, Buster and his father run from the Air Museum.

Buster and Blaster quickly tell Sparkplug everything.

"But our biggest problem still remains," says Sparkplug sadly. "Megatron knows about the Sun-Pak. He won't rest until he has found its secret."

"Don't worry about that," says Blaster. "Just before I transmitted the tape, I made certain changes in it. I erased all mention of the Sun-Pak."

"But Starscream and Bombshell know about it," says Buster.

"Starscream is no problem. Once he's reprogrammed, he'll be lucky to remember his own name. And as for Bombshell...in order to tell Megatron about the Sun-Pak, he would have to admit his part in the treason," says Blaster. "Somehow, I don't think even an Insecticon is stupid enough to do that. Our secret is safe, good friends. It looks like the Insecticon is caught by his own sting!"

THE END

"All right," says Buster. "Prepare to receive the taped transmission."

Blaster rewinds the tape, then sends it high-speed to Megatron. Now all the human and Autobot can do is wait—and hope.

The minutes tick by. Buster leaves his corner and watches as Bombshell finishes preparing his cerebroshell.

"You have one minute, human," the evil Insecticon says to Sparkplug. "Give us the secret of the Sun-Pak now—or prepare to become our slave forever!"

"I will never give in!" Sparkplug says bravely. But Buster can see that his father is pale.

"It's too late," Buster whispers to Blaster. "We'll have to—"

But at that moment the deafening roar of jet engines fills the Air Museum and a voice thunders, "Megatron calling Starscream!"

"It's Megatron!" gasps Starscream. "How did he find me?"

Turn to page 24.

Instantly Blaster fires his scrambler at Starscream. The Decepticon cries out in pain. "My circuits! My circuits!"

At the same instant Bumblebee crashes through the door. "Hold on, Buster!" he calls. There is a jolting *crash* just as Bombshell fires.

As Bumblebee hoped, the Insecticon's probe has missed its target.

Instead of shooting Sparkplug, Bombshell has shot Starscream!

And now the evil Decepticon looks around in confusion. "Where am I?" he asks. "Who are these people?"

Instantly Blaster realizes that Starscream's mind has been scrambled by the cerebro-shell. "We are your masters, Starscream," he says quickly. "Don't you remember? You made a mistake. You brought Sparkplug here without our permission. Now it's time that you returned him to us."

"Oh, no!" says Starscream. "I'm terribly sorry! How could I have done such a thing!"

"Starscream, you idiot!" cries Bombshell. "They are lying! The human belongs to us!"

Go on to page 29.

Starscream ignores Bombshell. "Is this insect annoying you, Masters?" he asks. "If so, I could swat it for you."

"That won't be necessary," says Blaster. "Just let us have the human."

"With pleasure," says Starscream. Gently, he brushes dust off Sparkplug's jacket. "Go with your friends now," he says. "I'm terribly sorry if I caused you any inconvenience."

Buster, Sparkplug, Blaster, and Bumblebee roar off toward Autobot headquarters. They're safe and so is the plan for the Sun-Pak. As they speed away they hear angry screams coming from the museum. No matter what Bombshell tries to tell him, Starscream insists that he works for the Autobots!

Bombshell's furious screams can be heard for miles, filling the air with deafening anger. But for the four friends, it's music to their ears!

THE END

"I have a plan," says Mirage. "How fast can you run?"

"I'm on the varsity track team," says Buster. "What do you want me to do?"

"I'm going to use my electro-disrupter to confuse the Insecticons. While they are busy with me, I want you to run in and grab the Sun-Pak. Then run out just as fast."

"No problem," says Buster.

"Just be careful. If we fail, nothing will save us."

Mirage activates his electro-disrupter. Instantly an image that looks just like him appears on the far side of the clearing. "Hey, insect-brains!" he calls out.

The Insecticons stop their discussion and turn to look.

"It's an Autobot!" cries Shrapnel.

"Not for long!" cries Bombshell. "It's about to become scrap metal!" He aims and fires. The shell explodes harmlessly against a tree trunk.

"I said over *here*!" says Mirage. He now seems to be on the other side! Again Bombshell fires—and again misses.

"Behind you, bug-brain!" says Mirage.

Turn to page 67.

The blasts of lasers, cluster bombs, and sonic booms continue to shake the cavern. Rising dust makes it hard to see what is happening.

Still, the Autobots fight on.

"Taste the fury of my machine guns!" cries Dirge. He aims at Ironhide and fires.

"What's that?" says Ironhide. "You want to tickle me? Well, chew on this for a while, you two-bit bucket of bolts!" He aims his power nozzle and prepares to shoot superheated lead at the evil Decepticon.

But his energy is almost exhausted. A high *ping-ping-ping* announces that the Sun-Pak is out of power. Instead of molten lead, all that comes out of the nozzle is harmless steam.

"Optimus Prime!" cries Ratchet. "Ironhide is in trouble!"

"I'm afraid we all are," says Optimus Prime sadly. "You are all brave. But even the bravest Autobot can run out of power. We have fought well. But we must retreat."

Turn to page 40.

Optimus Prime and the others pull up at the entrance to the deadly forest. At that moment Mirage and Buster come out of hiding. "The Decepticons are in there—in a clearing," Mirage whispers to Optimus Prime. "They are preparing an ambush."

"Is that right?" says Optimus Prime. "Well, let's see if we can turn their plan around. Ironhide, how much corrosive acid can you shoot?"

"A lot," says the van. "I'm fully recharged."

"Then come over here," says Optimus Prime. "The Decepticons must be very crowded in there. A little bit of acid should go a long way."

"This should be as easy as shooting pickles in a barrel," says Ironhide. Still in his van form, he drives to the entrance of the clearing. Quietly he inserts his nozzle through the tangled branches. Then he begins to shoot a stream of powerful acid into the clearing. Almost immediately there are screams of pain from inside.

"*Aargh!* My joints!" cries Starscream's voice.

"Help! My manifold is disintegrating!" cries Thundercracker.

"What's happening?" shrieks Kickback. "I can't see!"

Turn to page 45.

Before Optimus Prime can take action, Shrapnel presses a button on a black box. Immediately, the air vibrates with a terrible noise.

"It's an electro-disrupter!" gasps Ratchet.

"Your power is pitifully low," sneers Shrapnel. "You don't have the strength to withstand the disrupter. You won't even be able to move.... This will hold you while I go off and transmit my find to Megatron. He will reward me well for this!" Laughing evilly, he goes off to another canyon where the Insecticons are camped.

The Autobots are almost out of power. They are getting weaker by the minute.

"No...strength..." gasps Mirage. "Optimus... what can we do?"

"We must...try to fight," says the once-powerful leader.

"Wait!" says Sparkplug. "There may be a better way. Ironhide, is the Sun-Pak still intact?"

"Yes," says Ironhide. "But...out of power...."

Quickly Sparkplug removes the Sun-Pak from Ironhide's fuel feed. "I can change the wiring on the battery," he says. "I can rig it to give all Autobots full power for one hour. The only problem is we need to charge it in the sun."

Go on to page 35.

34

The Autobots look gloomily at one another. They are deep within the mountain. There seems to be no way to get to the surface. The Autobots are unable to move—and the humans are too small and weak.

"Maybe I can help," says Beachcomber. "I'm pretty weak, but I need less fuel than you big guys. And my geological functions are still working. If I can get away from the disrupter, I . . . I . . . could reach the surface."

"You're too weak!" gasps Ratchet. "It would be suicide!"

"Besides," says Ironhide, "we must keep the Sun-Pak here. We may be able to bargain with it."

The buzzing of the Insecticons grows louder. Obviously more Insecticons are coming. Optimus Prime must make a decision now. Megatron and his forces must be on their way. The Autobots are too weak to fight. But Beachcomber may not be able to charge the Sun-Pak in time. The only other hope is to somehow make a deal with the Insecticons. What should Optimus Prime do?

. . . .

If you think he should let Beachcomber try to reach the surface with the Sun-Pak, turn to page 53.

If you think he should keep the Sun-Pak and try to make a deal with the Insecticons, turn to page 38.

The battle between Optimus Prime and Megatron continues. But now Megatron scores a lucky hit. With horror, Optimus Prime realizes that his fuel line has been nicked. He is losing fuel!

Megatron notices his opponent's growing weakness. "Had enough, Prime?" he snarls.

Optimus Prime hates to admit defeat. But if he continues to fight he may be damaged permanently. Sadly, he lifts his hands in surrender and crawls over to the rock with the Sun-Pak.

Megatron follows, laughing cruelly. "Coward!" he sneers.

Suddenly Optimus Prime appears to trip. He falls, and his laser rifle fires. It hits the booby trap surrounding the Sun-Pak. When the smoke has cleared, the Sun-Pak is in a million tiny pieces.

"Cheat!" cries Megatron. "Filthy Autobot! I'll get you for this!" He is furious. He knows he has lost all hope of learning the secrets of the Sun-Pak.

Optimus Prime joins the rest of the Autobots, who are on the road back to Autobot headquarters. Cheers ring out when they see him! Optimus Prime can't help laughing at how well his trick worked. And he resolves that the first thing he will do when he gets back is ask Sparkplug to make another Sun-Pak!

"Yes," says Optimus Prime with a smile. "This was definitely a good trip."

THE END

"It's too dangerous for you to leave, Beach-comber. Let's try to make a deal with the Insecticons!" Optimus Prime says.

"So, you want to make a deal, do you?" a voice says nastily. It is Shrapnel. "I have heard every word you said, Optimus Prime. The electro-disrupter beamed your voices directly into my receiver."

"What do you want, Shrapnel?" demands Optimus Prime.

"Want? I want everything! I want the Sun-Pak, the humans, and you! I have brought Bombshell with me. Come here, Bombshell." Shrapnel gestures, and the Insecticon they call Bombshell approaches. His metallic skin shines in the dim light. "My cerebro-shell will deliver you into our hands!" he tells Optimus Prime. "Once I have shot you with it, you and all the Autobots will be slaves of the Insecticons!"

"Never!" cries Optimus Prime. He starts to struggle. Shrapnel presses another button on the electro-disrupter. Almost immediately Optimus Prime and all the Autobots stop moving.

"He's turned it to full power!" whispers Spark-plug. He and Buster are hidden behind Optimus Prime. "The Autobots are helpless!"

"Then it's up to us," whispers Buster. "What if we grabbed the disrupter? Could you figure out how to work it?"

"It seems to be a simple device," says Sparkplug. "Besides, it's our only chance."

Turn to page 61.

"I'll inject you with one of my cerebro-shells," chuckles the evil Insecticon. "No one—human or robot—can withstand their power. Your mind will be in our control—forever!"

"Think it over," says Starscream. "Either tell me voluntarily, or we use the cerebro-shell. You can decide while my friend here prepares the cerebro-shell."

"We've got to do something!" says Buster.

"There isn't time to send for the Autobots," says Blaster. "And I'm not sure my electro-scrambler will work on both of them."

"Then let's go get Bumblebee!" says Buster. "He can help."

"Yes, but remember, he isn't armed," says Blaster. "But I have an idea. I have just recorded Starscream's plans to take over the Decepticons. What if we gave this information to Megatron? Megatron will destroy Starscream for us!"

Now Buster and Blaster must make a decision.

....

If you think they should try to contact Megatron, turn to page 14.

If you think they have a better chance by getting Bumblebee's help, turn to page 70.

Optimus Prime knows that a good leader must know when to retreat. Right now he must think of the safety of the Autobots and the humans.

"Bumblebee," he orders, "take the humans and enter the tunnel you found. The rest of the Autobots follow. Quick! I'll hold off the Decepticons as long as I can."

Bumblebee and the other Autobots do as they are ordered. When Optimus Prime sees that all his troops are safe, he follows them. Then he sets off a dynamite charge. It collapses the entrance to the passage. The Decepticons cannot follow.

Quickly the Autobots begin to roll toward the surface and to safety. But suddenly they come to a fork. Instead of one tunnel, there are now two! There is no way to tell which tunnel leads to the surface.

The left-hand tunnel is steep and narrow. The right-hand passage is wider. But there are strange buzzing sounds coming from it.

Which tunnel should Optimus Prime choose?

If you think he should take the right-hand tunnel, turn to page 6.

If you think the left-hand tunnel is safer, turn to page 66.

"We can't take any chances," says Optimus Prime. "The Sun-Pak is too important. We must return to base and refuel."

A few hours later all the Autobots have refueled and are at full power.

"Autobots, transform!" commands their leader.

In a few seconds all the Autobots have transformed into their vehicle forms, and the impressive convoy rolls out on the road to Decepticon headquarters.

Just before they arrive, an alarm begins to shriek. The Decepticon spy, Ravage, was out patrolling. He has seen them!

The area begins to shake with the noise of jet engines. One by one, the Decepticons fly out from their headquarters. Commanding them is their towering leader, Megatron.

"How dare you attack us?" demands the evil robot.

"We don't want to attack anybody," says Optimus Prime. "You have something that belongs to us. Return the Sun-Pak and we will go peacefully."

. . . .

Turn to page 42.

"Don't make me laugh, Prime!" says Megatron. "You have ten seconds to turn around. If you don't, you and all the Autobots will be a pool of melted microchips!"

Optimus Prime expected a fight. The Autobots are ready! "Autobots, defend yourselves!" he commands. Quickly he aims his laser rifle and fires.

Just as quickly Megatron fires back. In the next minute the area around Decepticon headquarters becomes a battleground. Laser blasts, cluster bombs, and sonic charges go off everywhere. The earth shakes from the force of the explosions!

There is a shriek of torn metal and the Decepticon Thundercracker goes down. A cry of triumph tells Optimus Prime that an armor-piercing rocket from Mirage has hit its mark. But a moment later Mirage himself is down, the victim of Buzzsaw's mortar cannon.

Optimus Prime fires at Buzzsaw with his laser rifle. Everywhere around him Autobots and Decepticons are locked in battle. Many Autobots and many Decepticons are hurt.

Turn to page 44.

42

Neither side can win this battle, thinks Optimus Prime. I must do something to break the standoff.

At that moment Bumblebee approaches.

"Get back!" cries Optimus Prime. "It's not safe for you here! You're too small!"

"I've found the Sun-Pak!" Bumblebee says quickly. "It is being charged in the sun right now. But it is surrounded by booby traps!"

"You've done well," says Optimus Prime. "Now get to safety while I decide what to do."

Optimus Prime thinks for a moment. He realizes there are two things he can do to end the standoff.

He can concentrate his full fighting power on Megatron. If he can defeat their leader, the other Decepticons will probably give up.

Or he can forget about trying to defeat the Decepticons. Instead, he can try to capture the Sun-Pak.

Which should Optimus Prime do?

If you think Optimus Prime should go one-on-one against Megatron, turn to page 16.

If you think he should make a grab for the Sun-Pak, turn to page 57.

"Decepticons, transform!" cries Megatron. "Our ambush has turned out to be a trap—for us!"

In a panic the Decepticons pour out of the forest. Most of them are damaged. Though badly injured, they begin to fly away.

The Autobots give a cheer.

"Well done, Ironhide," says Optimus Prime. "Now let's get the Sun-Pak."

Optimus Prime and Ironhide enter the forest. A few minutes later they return. "I have good news and bad news," Optimus Prime tells his troops. "The good news is that the Decepticons didn't get the Sun-Pak."

"What's the bad news?" asks Mirage.

"The bad news is that Ironhide did!"

Optimus Prime holds up a formless mess of metal and fiberglass. "This is all that remains of the original Sun-Pak," he says. "It was in the direct line of fire of Ironhide's nozzle. I'm almost sorry now that Megatron didn't take it with him!"

The Autobots laugh cheerfully. They know Sparkplug will soon produce another Sun-Pak. And for this moment at least, their future seems bright.

THE END

"No, we can't go along with Megatron. If we play him the tape now, we'll have nothing left to bargain with," says Buster.

"I'm afraid you're right," says Blaster. "Come, let's return to your father. There may still be time to help him."

Back in the main hall they hear Starscream's evil cackle. "Your time is up, human!" he says to Spark-plug. "Now prepare to receive the cerebro-shell!"

Bombshell approaches Sparkplug slowly. Buster whispers frantically to Blaster, "We've got to do some-thing!"

At that moment the air is split by a scream of jets landing. A few seconds later Megatron, backed up by the Decepticon force, appears in the doorway of the Air Museum.

"Carrying out a private experiment, Starscream?" the towering robot asks.

Starscream is startled, but he recovers quickly. "An experiment to strengthen your power, O Mighty Megatron," he says. Starscream explains about the Sun-Pak. "This foolish human will not give us the secret," he finishes. "We were just about to make him more cooperative."

"You had no right to act on your own!" says Megatron. "But the Decepticons must have the Sun-Pak, so proceed. I'll deal with your behavior later!"

"No!" cries Buster from his hiding place. "What about the tape, Megatron? I have evidence—"

Go on to page 47.

"Silence, human!" thunders Megatron. "What do I care about your tape when I can have the secret of the Sun-Pak? Starscream is under my control. Now leave here immediately, or you will taste the cerebro-shell yourself!"

At that moment there is an agonizing scream from Sparkplug. To his horror, Buster sees that his father has been injected with the cerebro-shell.

"What is your bidding, O Megatron?" asks Sparkplug. "I will do whatever Your Mightiness asks."

Buster starts to run toward his father. But Blaster tells him to stop. "We can't help Sparkplug now. The only thing we can do is take this sad news to Autobot headquarters before the Decepticons get us, too."

Turn to page 60.

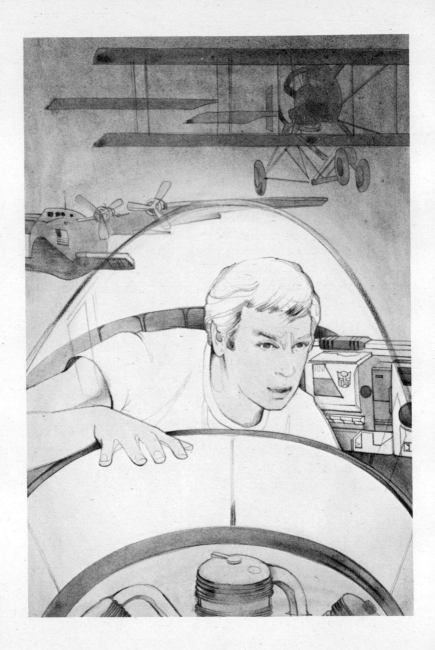

For the rest of the afternoon they hide in an old two-engine plane. Buster is worried and distressed about his father, so Blaster tries to relax him by playing Buster's favorite rock group, Purple Fungus. He lets him listen on earphones.

At last the museum closes, and Starscream transforms!

Then the Insecticon Bombshell climbs out of a World War II fighter plane. He is carrying Sparkplug. The human is tied up and has a gag in his mouth.

Starscream laughs gleefully. "With the Sun-Pak I will no longer need fuel," he says. "At long last, the Decepticons will obey me as their rightful leader!"

Bombshell smiles, then removes Sparkplug's gag. "Tell us the plans for the Sun-Pak, human," he says.

"Never!" says Sparkplug. "I'll die first."

"That could be arranged," says Starscream. "But it won't be necessary. Fortunately, Bombshell here has a way to change your mind."

Turn to page 39.

For a moment there is shocked silence in the cave. Then Buster realizes what has happened. "My father!" Buster cries. "The Decepticons have kidnapped Sparkplug!"

"Those filthy Decepticons," says Ironhide. "I'll—"

"You'll do nothing," says Ratchet. "Your powers are depleted."

"*I* still have plenty of fuel," says Bumblebee. "Come on, Buster, let's go find him!" Bumblebee may be the smallest Autobot, but he's always big on courage!

"I'm coming too," says Blaster. "It's about time Starscream faced the music!"

"The rest of the Autobots will refuel," says Optimus Prime. "When you have found Sparkplug, radio Autobot headquarters. We'll come at once!"

The other Autobots prepare to return to headquarters. And Blaster prepares to go with Buster. In three seconds he has transformed. He now looks like a tape deck. He and Buster get inside Bumblebee's car body and set off in the direction of Decepticon headquarters.

Buster looks up at the sky. "There is no sign of them," he says.

Go on to page 51.

"Don't worry," says Blaster. "My sensors can detect the smallest radio transmission. Starscream's a blabbermouth. I'll pick him up soon." In the next instant there is a high-pitched whining noise. "That's him!" he says. "Bumblebee, turn right!"

"But Decepticon headquarters is in the other direction!" says Bumblebee.

"Maybe so, but I'm getting a transmission from Starscream. It's definitely on the right."

Bumblebee turns right. Soon he and his passengers are on the outskirts of a large city. There are a few houses with thick, green lawns, and a few larger buildings.

The high-pitched whining has become a scream. "Stop, Bumblebee," says Blaster. "We're there."

"Where's there?" says Bumblebee. "As near as I can tell, we're in the middle of some suburb. There's no sign of Starscream or any other Decepticon."

"The transmissions indicate he is quite close."

"Look!" says Buster. He points to a sign. It says AIR MUSEUM—AUTHENTIC FIGHTER PLANES.

Turn to page 68.

For hours the battle between Optimus Prime and Megatron continues. Night falls, and still the giant robots continue to fight. The flashes of laser and fusion weapons light the dark sky. At last, nearly twelve hours after the battle began, Megatron begins to weaken.

"Give up, Megatron," says Optimus Prime. "You are nearly out of fuel!"

"Never!" cries Megatron. But Optimus Prime scores a direct hit. The evil Decepticon drops to the ground. Optimus Prime calls to Ratchet, who stayed in the shadows, unseen. Quickly Ratchet disarms the bombs around the Sun-Pak.

"It's a good thing Megatron ran out of power," says Optimus Prime. "That battle was the most exhausting one I've ever fought. I'm not sure I have enough power to roll home."

"Is that so?" says Ratchet. "In that case, I've got just the thing for you."

As the Autobots roll back to headquarters, a big semi-truck is in the lead. It is Optimus Prime, as powerful as he was twelve hours ago. He has not refueled—but beneath his hood is the fully recharged Sun-Pak. "Great idea, Ratchet," he says. "I've never felt stronger. In fact, I can't wait for our next battle with the Decepticons!"

THE END

"Beachcomber, you may be our best hope," says Optimus Prime. "Go now."

"I promise I will not fail you," says Beachcomber. "Give me the battery, Sparkplug. I'll be back as soon as I can."

The other Autobots shield Beachcomber with their bodies. The Insecticons do not see him even as he drives by the canyon where they are camped.

Once Beachcomber is away from the disrupter, his strength returns. He checks his seismic and magnetic sensors, and wriggles upward. Soon his sensors tell him that another passage lies beyond a pile of rubble. Using a geologist's electronic pick, he quickly cuts through the rock.

Now he finds himself in a small cavern. His infrared sensors show him sparkling gems. Below him is a stream full of strange white fish with no eyes. He would like to stay and appreciate the beauty for a moment, but duty sends him on.

Turn to page 71.

Beachcomber seals the Sun-Pak in a waterproof bag. Then he splashes into the shallow pool.

Around him colorful fish swim. His sensors lead him to an underground stream. He enters the stream and follows it. It twists and turns.

I should have taken the other path, he thinks. Just then, the stream breaks into open air.

Beachcomber looks up. Above him the sun is shining in a bright blue sky.

Quickly he climbs out of the stream. He places the Sun-Pak on a flat, dry rock. He sets its controls to "Charge." Then he stretches out by the rock. While the battery is charging, he looks at the mountains and trees.

"This is a magnificent planet," he says to himself. "I wish I could just sit here and study it for days."

But soon a buzzing sound tells him his peaceful time is over. A dark shadow passes over him. He looks up and sees Kickback, the Insecticon!

Turn to page 23.

54

"We accept your surrender!" says Optimus Prime. "Order your troops to withdraw!"

Starscream continues to fly around the cave in erratic circles. Smokescreen's magnetic missiles have caused him to lose all control. At last he gasps out the order to withdraw.

But then, suddenly, Thundercracker and the other Decepticons turn on Starscream.

"Coward!" cries Thundercracker. "Decepticons do not surrender!" A barrage of bombs, rockets, and energy bolts blasts the already weakened Decepticon.

"Nooo—" cries Starscream. But his anguished cry ends abruptly. The Autobots step back as what is left of Starscream explodes with a loud *whoosh! kablam!*

"As for you Autobots," sneers Thundercracker, "you are safe for now. I must report this treason to Megatron. He will decide when and how to deal with you!"

With that, the evil Decepticons transform and fly out of the cave. Optimus Prime is happy to see them go—especially since they were kind enough to destroy Starscream for him.

"Hey," says Ironhide, "with enemies like them, who needs friends?"

"We do," says Optimus Prime, looking over his loyal troops as they all head home.

THE END

The wise leader of the Autobots decides to go for the Sun-Pak.

The battle continues to rage. Optimus Prime begins to move toward the edge of the battlefield. After a moment he sees the Sun-Pak, recharging in the sun. It is exactly where Bumblebee said it would be, surrounded by a tangle of thermite bombs.

"Smokescreen," he calls to his friend, "do you think your disrupter rifle could disable those bombs?"

"No problem," says Smokescreen.

But he is knocked to the ground by a sudden blast. Now Megatron's voice booms, "Not so fast, Prime! I see what you're up to. But you won't get the Sun-Pak! When it's charged I'm going to add it to my power supply!"

Optimus Prime shudders. No matter what else happens, he must prevent that from happening.

But how? Megatron is now standing in front of the booby-trapped Sun-Pak. His fusion cannons will blast anyone who tries to get near the battery.

"I have an idea," Smokescreen whispers. Optimus Prime listens, then he laughs.

"Go right ahead, old friend," he says. "Transform!"

Turn to page 73.

Soon the other Autobots are out of the tunnel and on the road to headquarters. "Hey," says Sparkplug, "where is Ironhide?"

Quickly Optimus Prime goes back to the bottom of the tunnel. He returns a few minutes later with Ironhide, who is out cold.

Ratchet works on Ironhide with a portable emergency generator. Before long, the old Autobot comes to and transforms to his robot form. Weakly, he tells his friends what has happened.

"The Insecticons have the Sun-Pak!" says Mirage. "Let's track those beady-eyed bugs now!"

"We're too low on power," says Ratchet. "We must return to headquarters first to refuel."

Now Optimus Prime must make a decision. What should he do?

If you think he should have all the Autobots return to base and refuel first, turn to page 41.

If you think he should save time by sending an advance scout after the Sun-Pak, turn to page 65.

Mirage cannot help laughing. "So long, sharp-shooters!" he says. "Hope you enjoyed the target practice as much as we did!"

Still laughing, he joins Buster outside the forest. "Boy, I'd love to see Megatron's face when he gets here and there's no Sun-Pak!" Mirage says. Buster holds the Sun-Pak in his hand—and that's no illusion. Off they speed to a real victory!

THE END

For the next several weeks the Autobots wait anxiously for the dreaded news that the Decepticons have the Sun-Pak.

But, strangely, that never happens.

It is only much later, on a routine espionage mission, that Mirage discovers the reason. Under the influence of the cerebro-shell, Sparkplug tried to reproduce the Sun-Pak for the Decepticons. But no matter how hard he worked, he couldn't seem to do it. Apparently, the cerebro-shell temporarily damaged part of his memory. The Decepticons were so disgusted, they let him go.

"It wasn't a total loss for the Decepticons, though," a recovered Sparkplug tells the others later. "I did manage to create a new invention for them. It's a portable laser-operated toothbrush. Too bad the Decepticons don't have teeth!"

THE END

Bombshell approaches Optimus Prime and prepares to fire the cerebro-shell. Shrapnel watches. Neither notices as the humans stealthily draw nearer.

"Ready," says Shrapnel, "aim..."

"Look out, Shrapnel!" yells Buster. Startled, the Insecticon turns to look at Buster. At the same moment Sparkplug grabs the electro-disrupter. He aims it at Shrapnel and presses two buttons at once. Shrapnel screams in pain and then falls silent. He and the other Insecticon become motionless.

"Are you all right?" Sparkplug asks Optimus Prime.

"That was a close call," says Optimus Prime. "Thank you!"

"No thanks necessary," says Sparkplug. "I think Shrapnel forgot that humans don't have electronic circuits. He didn't realize we were unaffected by the disrupter."

Optimus Prime takes the Sun-Pak and guards it himself. "Autobots, roll out!" he calls. One by one, the Autobots transform and begin to climb out of the canyon. Behind them, the Insecticons remain motionless—and helpless.

"Well, I guess there's some advantage to being human after all," Sparkplug says.

"Yeah, I gotta hand it to you, Sparkplug," Ironhide agrees. "You do pretty well, even without four-wheel drive!"

THE END

No! It's not the end! Suddenly a shot rings out and Kickback is hit! The grasshopper-like creature looks around in shock. Who is firing at him?

That's what Beachcomber wonders too! Then he sees an amazing sight. It's Sparkplug Witwicky—and Buster is right behind him.

"How did you get here?" Beachcomber asks.

"We just couldn't stay there and do nothing!" Sparkplug says. "We had to do something, so we followed you. But we took a strange turn and found a real shortcut. We can get back to the Insecticons' nest by going under a hidden waterfall. Come on. Grab the Sun-Pak, Buster. I hope we're not too late to save our friends!"

Turn to page 64.

Beachcomber puts the charged Sun-Pak back in the waterproof bag. Then Sparkplug leads him to a waterfall. Beneath the waterfall is a secret passage that leads right to the Insecticons' nest. It takes them only minutes to get there.

Amazing! When they get there, the Autobots are still alive, still held in place by the disrupter. Shrapnel is still trying to make contact with Megatron.

"The cave-in must have interfered with their communications," Sparkplug whispers. "Lucky for us."

Beachcomber, Sparkplug, and Buster silently sneak back to where the weak Autobots are held. Sparkplug changes the wiring on the battery and, one by one, the Autobots secretly recharge.

When they are at full power, the disrupter isn't strong enough to hold them.

"AUTOBOTS, ATTACK!" Optimus Prime yells.

Turn to page 74.

"I need a volunteer to go after the Sun-Pak," says Optimus Prime gravely.

"I still have a few hours' worth of fuel," says Mirage. "Let me follow Shrapnel. We can't let him escape with the Sun-Pak!"

Optimus Prime nods. "A good point, Mirage. But I can't send one Autobot alone against the Insecticons."

"I'll go along," says Buster. "I don't need fuel. And two heads are better than one."

Optimus thinks a moment. "If this weren't such a desperate situation, I would refuse," he says. "But you can both go on one condition. You must promise that you will go as scouts—only scouts. If you find the Sun-Pak, you will radio for help. You won't try to do anything on your own."

"But what if—" says Mirage.

"No buts!" says Optimus. "Promise me."

"I promise," says Mirage.

"Me too," says Buster.

The other Autobots roll off in the direction of headquarters. Mirage spends a moment adjusting his electronic sensors. "I detect a strange insectlike buzzing on the ultrasonic frequencies," he says. "Let's follow it."

Turn to page 19.

"We'll take the tunnel on the left. Bumblebee, lead the way," commands Optimus Prime.

Soon the Autobots are rolling toward—they hope—the surface.

"It's really narrow here," says Bumblebee. "It's going to be a tight fit for you big guys."

Unfortunately, Bumblebee is right. Ironhide, who is almost out of power, gets stuck at a turn in the tunnel.

"Nuts!" he grumbles. He is too embarrassed to call for help. He revs his engine and rocks back and forth, trying to get loose.

And then he hears a sound that chills his transmission fluid. It is the buzzing of a scarab beetle. In his small insect form, Shrapnel has followed him. And now the evil Insecticon lands on his body just above the Sun-Pak.

"Bug off!" says Ironhide, but Shrapnel only chuckles.

Aiming his antennae carefully, Shrapnel disrupts the Sun-Pak's electronic lock. Then he takes the Sun-Pak and prepares to fly off.

"So long, Autobot," he sneers. "Next time we meet, I will be unstoppable!"

Turn to page 58.

By now Bombshell is so confused and angry he can scarcely aim. The other Insecticons join the fight.

"Shrapnel, watch your back!" laughs Mirage. When Shrapnel turns around, Mirage has vanished again.

Angrily, Shrapnel aims his grenade launcher. He has forgotten all about the Sun-Pak.

This is Buster's chance! While Mirage continues to throw images of himself all over the forest, he starts to run. The Insecticons do not even notice him. He grabs the Sun-Pak and runs out of the forest.

Back in the clearing, Mirage creates one more illusion. He projects his appearance in six directions at once. "Here I am!" he shouts. His voice seems to come from everywhere. "Catch me if you can!"

The frenzied Insecticons all begin firing at once.

"*Aaargh!*" cries Bombshell. "You hit me, Shrapnel!"

"Be careful!" calls Kickback. "You almost got me with your—*owwww!*"

Soon all the Insecticons are lying on the ground, wounded by their own weapons.

Turn to page 59.

"Could be," says Bumblebee. "But why would Starscream hide in a museum?"

"Let's find out!" says Blaster.

"I'm sorry we have to leave you here," says Buster to Bumblebee.

"I don't mind," says the little Autobot. "I'll be right here in the parking lot if you need my help."

Buster carries Blaster to the museum entrance.

"A dollar fifty," says the attendant. He looks bored. But then he frowns. "Hey, kid," he says. "I see you've got one of those cassette players. No music in the museum!"

"I won't play it," Buster promises.

Inside the walls of the museum there are a dozen planes. Some are very old, with propellers instead of jets. Some are very new and modern looking. It takes only a moment to spot Starscream.

"There he is!" says Buster. "But where is my father?"

"I don't know," says Blaster. "Let's wait till the museum closes. I have a hunch we'll find out what Starscream is up to then."

Turn to page 49.

What should Optimus Prime do now? His natural sense of fair play tells him to accept Starscream's surrender. But on the other hand, trusting a Decepticon seems like a sure route to the junk pile.

....

If you think Optimus Prime should accept the surrender, turn to page 56.

If you think Optimus Prime should forget about his sense of fair play and let Smokescreen finish off the evil Decepticon, turn to page 10.

Quickly Blaster and Buster leave the museum and explain the situation to Bumblebee.

"There's no time to send for help," Buster finishes. "We've got to stop Bombshell before he uses his cerebro-shell on my father!"

"It's a desperate situation," says Blaster. "I can use my electro-scrambler gun. But I don't think it's powerful enough to stop both Starscream and Bombshell."

"I have an idea," says Bumblebee. "Turn your scrambler on Starscream. That should confuse him. Then I'll ram into Bombshell as he fires. That may make him miss. Then, if we move quickly, we can grab Sparkplug and make a run for it."

All three know that it is a desperate chance, but there seems to be no choice. Bumblebee positions himself right outside the door to the museum. Buster and Blaster go inside.

Back inside the museum, Bombshell is taking aim. "Foolish human," says the Insecticon. "Now you will be in our power forever."

Sparkplug is trembling, but he does not say a word.

Bombshell aims and prepares to fire.

"Now!" cries Buster.

Turn to page 28.

Beachcomber's sensors show him two possible routes to the surface. One is just ahead of him. The other leads downward into the pool of water. Which path should he choose?

If you think Beachcomber should take the path ahead of him, turn to page 21.

If you think he has a better chance by driving through the pool, turn to page 54.

71

Slowly the wounded Smokescreen transforms into the form of a race car. Then the small race car begins to rev his engine. After a moment, thick black smoke comes out of his tailpipe. The smoke twists and swirls. Soon it is so thick that it...blots out the sun!

"You miserable motorized moron!" cries Megatron. "What have you done? The Sun-Pak cannot be recharged now! But at least *you* won't get it!"

Megatron rips out the wiring for the bombs. Then he picks up the Sun-Pak and throws it to Buzzsaw. But Optimus Prime is too quick. He leaps after the Sun-Pak and catches it midair! "Autobots, roll out!" he yells.

"Hey, wait a minute!" screams Megatron, turning in the thick smoke. "Come back here with that!"

But he is too late. The Autobots have disappeared.

"Hey, Smokescreen," says Bumblebee as they roar toward home, "you were really smokin' today!"

THE END

The Sun-Pak gives the Autobots more than enough power to defeat the Insecticons. "Take that, you bugs," Bumblebee shouts as the last Insecticon falls.

Later, rolling home, the Autobots are happy and excited as they talk about their victory. They have a lot to be happy about! They escaped from the Decepticons. They defeated the Insecticons in their own nest—and they have the Sun-Pak. Or to put it another way—this is a victory they all really got a "charge" out of.

THE END